Chiquita's Children

Teaching Children about Foster Families

by Jan Wolff and Cheryl Hanson, RN, LP
Illustrated by Lorraine Dey

New Horizon Press
Far Hills, New Jersey

Dedication

To those we have loved–
blood-related and otherwise–
who showed us the meaning of family.

Requests for permission should be addressed to:
New Horizon Press
P.O. Box 669
Far Hills, NJ 07931

Jan Wolff and Cheryl Hanson, RN, LP
    Chiquita's Children: Teaching Children about Foster Families

Cover Design and Interior Illustrations: Lorraine Dey
Interior Design: Charley Nasta

Library of Congress Control Number: 2015913634

ISBN-13 (paperback): 978-0-88282-516-8
ISBN-13 (eBook): 978-0-88282-517-5

SMALL HORIZONS
A Division of New Horizon Press

Printed in the U.S.A.

20 19 18 17 16   1 2 3 4 5

From the time she grew her first wing feathers, Chiquita the chicken wanted to raise a family.

"Not many of us get to raise a family nowadays," said Tamara the turkey, "but if that is what you want, I wish you luck."

"We all wish you luck," echoed the other barnyard animals. All except Golda the goose, who sometimes acted a little grumpy.

"Raising a family is no picnic," she hissed. "Children do all sorts of unexpected things. Like arguing in public and eating June bugs until they spit up in bed. Still, if that is what you want, I do wish you luck."

One morning, Chiquita woke up with a heavy feeling in her belly. She yawned and stretched and out popped her first egg.

"Look, everyone!" she crowed. "Soon I will have my very own family."

"Not many chickens get to raise their very own families," said the other barnyard animals, "but if that is what you want, we hope you get your wish."

Chiquita made a nest in the straw and rolled the egg into it. Then she fluffed her feathers and sat down on top of it, humming a tune as she thought about the downy baby she would soon be mothering.

The next day Farmer Olson came into the chicken coop and removed Chiquita's egg, but before she had much time to be sad, she had laid another one.

And so it went. Every day Chiquita laid another egg and every day Farmer Olson carried it away. The other barnyard animals shook their heads sadly. "Not many of us get to raise our very own families," they said. "It takes a lot of luck."

"I will NOT give up!" Chiquita promised and, sure enough, one morning Farmer Olson returned with a basket over his arm.

He walked around the coop, looking at each bird, until he came to Chiquita.

"This little hen seems determined," he said, placing a dozen large eggs beneath her wings. Some were white, some pale green and some blue. "I will let her sit on these."

Chiquita's heart was filled with joy. For weeks she left her nest only to stretch and eat. Every day she carefully turned each egg. But the summer days grew long and the chicken coop grew hot and stuffy.

"I miss being outside," she confided to Golda. "I miss scratching in the dirt and picking grasshoppers off the bushes and walking in the meadow and clucking with my friends."

"Well, that is just the way it is when you are raising babies," huffed Golda. "You had better enjoy your rest now, because once they are hatched you will not get a moment's peace. It will be 'Mama this' and 'Mama that' all day long and sometimes all night, too. Did you think it would be easy?"

Golda gave a final hiss, flapped her wing goodbye and waddled away.

Chiquita felt so lonely she hung her head. Then she heard voices coming toward the chicken coop and when she looked out, there were all her barnyard friends in a semicircle around the door.

"Surprise," they shouted. "It is a baby shower!"

"We do not have any fancy gifts," snorted Pong the pig, "but we each want to give you something. My gift is a story you can tell your babies."

He then oinked the tale of *The Three Little Pigs* and how they outwitted the big bad wolf.

One by one, the other animals took their turns.

First, Harry the horse whinnied "The Old Grey Mare (She Ain't What She Used To Be)" followed by Sophia the sheep bleating "Baa, Baa, Black Sheep" and Caroline the cow tap-dancing in circles all around the yard.

Finally, Beatrice the border collie wrapped it all up with a rousing rendition of "Bingo Was His Name-O" before standing on her hind legs, bowing, rolling over and playing dead.

The other animals snorted, neighed and mooed their approval and Chiquita clapped her wings and laughed until her wattles shook.

"More! More!" she shouted, but the afternoon was fading and her friends had to hurry back to their homes.

Chiquita dreaded the long night ahead, but soon Golda sat down next to her.

"I will stay here tonight to keep you company," Golda said. Before long, her loud snores vibrated through the coop.

As Chiquita sat quietly waiting for sleep to come, she recited the names she planned to give her babies, all of them starting with the letters C and H like her own.

There was Charley…and Chauncey…and Chester…and Chelsea…and Cheryl…and Charlotte.

Finally her head began to nod, but as she drifted off to sleep she felt a nudge against her side. Her eyelids popped open and there, with its busy paws in the nest, stood a weasel. Chiquita was so startled she could barely cluck.

"I beg your pardon!" Chiquita gasped. "Just who are you and what are you doing in my nest?"

The golden brown weasel looked at her with a smile as sweet as honey. "So very sorry to have scared you, my dear," she said. "I am your new neighbor, Wanda the weasel. I just dropped by to introduce myself and borrow a little something, as good neighbors often do."

"Then I guess I am happy to meet you," sputtered Chiquita, calming down and smoothing her feathers. The weasel seemed nice and Chiquita thought about how good it would be to have someone to talk with during the long night ahead. "What is it you want to borrow?" she asked.

"Oh, if it is not too much trouble, just a few of your eggs?" purred the weasel, showing her pointy teeth in a shifty grin.

"My eggs?" Chiquita replied. "But whatever would you want with my eggs? My eggs are my future family!"

"So they are," smiled Wanda. "I can see you and I are going to get along great. I have babies of my own, you see, and it seems they are always crying for something. They would love to see your eggs. Could I borrow a few to quiet down my babies?"

With a sudden WHOOOOSH and a hiss, Golda sailed straight at the weasel's head. Her wildly flapping wings fanned the night air and her big yellow feet stomped the straw.

"Chiquita, you foolish chicken, wise up!" she cried. "Wanda's babies do not just want to see your eggs. They want to *eat* them!"

"Mind your own business, Golda!" snarled Wanda.

But before she could say more, Golda pushed Wanda back to the open door.

With a few loud honks and a nip to the rear end, Golda chased Wanda straight out of the coop.

All that noise woke the other animals, who set up such a ruckus that Beatrice began to bark.

That caused Farmer Olson to bound out of the house in his underwear, waving his arms and shaking his fists.

He shouted, "We will get that wily weasel if it is the last thing we do! Right, Beatrice?"

Chiquita's heart was pounding so hard she could hardly breathe. "How could anyone be so bad?" she gasped. "I thought I had made a new friend, but all she wanted was to steal my eggs. Now I hate her!"

"Oh, Wanda is not so bad," said Golda. "She is only doing the same as you, trying to raise a family. Anyway, she must be lonely having everyone angry at her. You do not need to hate her. Just be careful when she is around.

"And believe me, she is not the only scary thing you will face while raising your family, Chiquita, so keep your eyes open. Except for now. Right now, just close your eyes and go back to sleep."

Golda yawned, settled her plump bottom into the straw and started snoring again.

After that, Chiquita slept each night with Golda by her side until, one hot summer night, Chiquita was awakened by strange movements around her feet. "Help!" she shrieked. "Wanda is back!"

"Nonsense," hissed Golda. "It is just your babies hatching. Now quiet down, wait until morning and you will see."

When Chiquita peeked under her wings the next morning, sure enough, twenty-four bright little eyes peeked back up at her.

"Congratulations!" said the other barnyard animals, looking at Chiquita's new brood. "We certainly wish you happiness!"

In a few days, Chiquita's babies were no longer content to stay in their nest.

"Take them for a walk," said Golda. "They will follow you, you will see."

All that day Chiquita walked around the barnyard with her new family.

When evening came, she returned to her nest and, just as Golda had promised, her babies followed, snuggling beneath her as the night grew cooler.

"I am the world's happiest hen," she crowed. "At last, I have my very own family."

Chiquita's new arrivals grew so quickly she could hardly keep up with them. *They are getting so big and strong-willed*, she worried. *And not one of them looks a thing like me.*

"How will I ever be able to raise all these children properly?" she asked.

The other barnyard animals exchanged concerned looks. "You are a good mother," Sophia the sheep said. "You will manage somehow. With luck."

That night a big thunderstorm struck. The chicken coop shook and Chiquita's beak chattered with fright, but the next morning the sun shone brightly and sparkling new puddles decorated the barnyard.

"Praise be! We made it through the night," said Chiquita with relief as she led her babies outside. "Now, you children..."

But when she turned around, the children were nowhere to be seen. "Children? Children!" she cackled, running around in search of her brood.

"Peep, peep," came their familiar voices, from the middle of the biggest puddle.

"Help! My children are drowning!" shrieked Chiquita.

"Calm down!" said Golda. "Your children are *not* drowning. They are swimming."

"But chickens cannot swim!" squawked Chiquita.

Tamara put her wing on Chiquita's shoulder.

"We all love our children so much, it is sometimes hard for us to see them as they really are," Tamara said.

"We want them to be like us, but often they are not. And it is just as well, because they are wonderful just the way they are. Now look at your children again and tell me what you see."

"They…they are ducks! That is why they can swim," gasped Chiquita, blinking her eyes. She could not believe what she was seeing and she began to cry.

"My children are not really family at all!" she sobbed. "They are not even chickens."

"But of course they are family," said Sophia. "You do not have to be blood-related to be family."

"Just look at all of us," nodded Pong. "We are different shapes, sizes and colors, but we help and love each other. If that is not family, I do not know what is."

Chiquita looked at all the different faces around her. *Why, they are right!* she thought. *How boring this world would be if we were all the same. It is the differences that make it so interesting.*

"My children may be ducks," Chiquita said, "but I am still their mother. I will always love them and they will always love me and they will live with me forever in our cozy nest."

The other barnyard animals looked at one another and smiled. "Not many children live with their parents all their lives," they said, "but if you are sure that is what you want, we wish you LOTS of luck."

Tips for Children

1. Do not be afraid to meet people who look or act differently from you.

2. If you have friends or classmates from another country, ask them what that country was like. How was it different from where they are living now?

3. If you have a chance, try some food that is commonly eaten in another country. You might find something you like or, if you do not like it right away, you might grow to like it.

4. Try to imagine how it would feel to be the only child in your class or play group who looks different from everyone else.

5. Learn a few words from another language, like "Hello," "Thank you" and "Goodbye." Use them when you can.

6. If someone you know does something you do not like, try to understand why they did it. Could it be that their life is so different from yours that they act in a way that is strange to you?

7. Look into your best friend's face. How is it different from your own? Notice that you are more alike than different.

8. Be aware of how each season of the year is beautiful in its own way. Enjoy the budding green trees of spring, the red, yellow, pink and purple flowers of summer, the golden leaves of autumn and the fluffy, white snow of winter.

9. Try to remember that when someone does something nice for you they are giving you a gift.

10. When you see a flower garden, observe the various shapes and colors that make it more beautiful than it would be if they were all the same.

Tips for Parents

1. Remember that children tend to adopt their parents' view of diversity.

2. Expose your child to different races and cultures as often as possible. Explain how we are all more similar than different.

3. If someone does something that is upsetting to your child, talk with the child about how it made him or her feel. Help him or her to understand that there might have been extenuating circumstances beyond the person's control.

4. If your child expresses fear of someone who is different, listen carefully to his or her fears and, if possible, allow him or her to gradually become acquainted with that person.

5. Encourage your child to include a child who is different in his or her activities as often as possible.

6. Teach your child to have empathy for someone who might be struggling with a disability, new language or culture. Talk about how those struggles might feel.

7. Help your child understand that if something does not turn out the way he or she wanted, it is not necessarily a bad thing.

8. Encourage your child to enjoy nature in all its various forms.

9. Remind your child that all gifts are not tangible.

10. Model and teach respect for all living things.